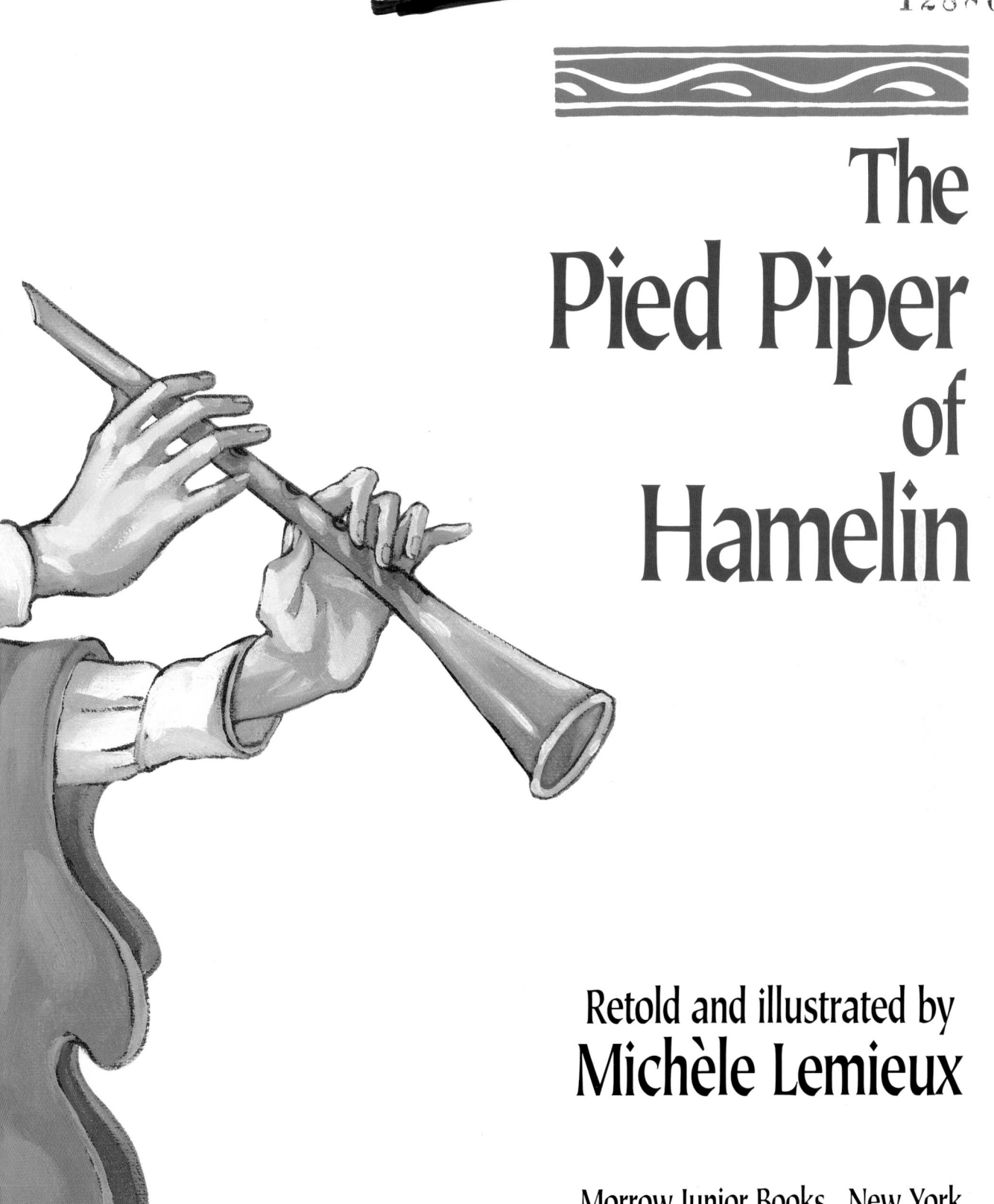

The Pied Piper of Hamelin

Retold and illustrated by
Michèle Lemieux

Morrow Junior Books   New York

Oil paints were used for the full-color art. The text type is 17-point Tiepolo Book.

Printed in Hong Kong by South China Printing Company (1988) Ltd.

1   2   3   4   5   6   7   8   9   10

Library of Congress Cataloging-in-Publication Data
Lemieux, Michèle.
The Pied Piper of Hamelin / retold and illustrated by Michèle Lemieux.   p.   cm.   Summary: The Pied
Piper pipes the village free of rats, and when the villagers refuse to pay him for the service, he exacts a
terrible revenge.
ISBN 0-688-09848-7.—ISBN 0-688-09849-5 (lib. bdg.)
1. Pied Piper of Hamelin (Legendary character)—Legends.
[1. Pied Piper of Hamelin (Legendary character)   2. Folklore—
Germany—Hamelin.]   I. Pied Piper of Hamelin.   II. Title.
PZ8.1.L4233Pi   1993   398.21—dc20   [E]   92-21338   CIP   AC

To my sister
Andrée

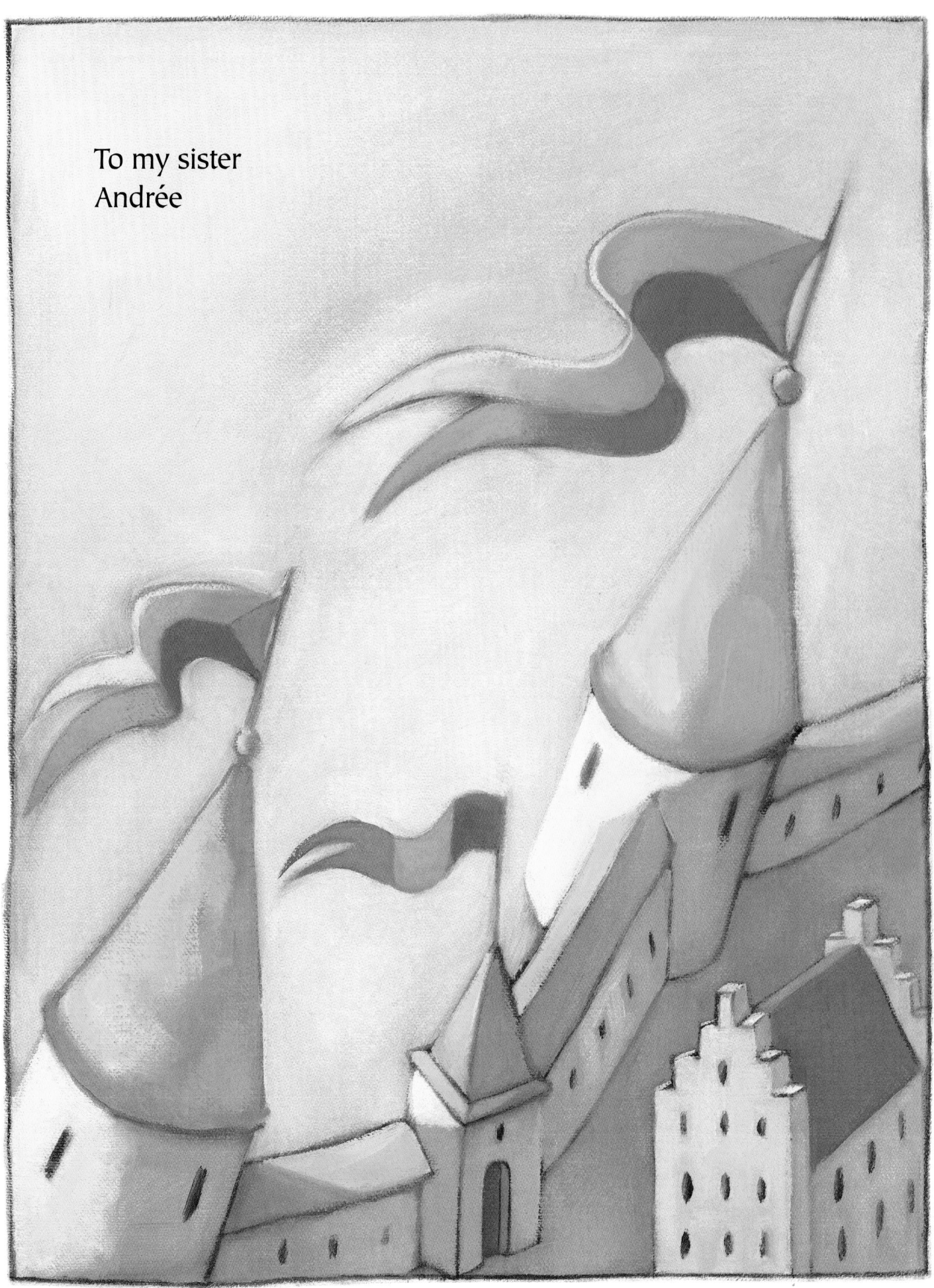

Life was easy for the people of Hamelin, a grand city on the banks of the river Weser. The poor were not too poor, and the rich had much more than they needed. But instead of being thankful, the townspeople were greedy and selfish. They showed no concern for others and

thought only of their own pleasures. The people were
blessed with many children, but the parents spent their
time eating and drinking; they felt that their children only
took up time and caused trouble.

Then one day something terrible happened in Hamelin....

On the day before Christmas in 1283, all the townspeople were busy preparing for the Christmas feast. Throughout the town, you could smell hams and turkeys roasting and cakes and pies baking. In all of the activity, no one noticed that a rat had slipped through the town gates. It was followed by another, and then another. Within five minutes there were a hundred rats; after an hour there were more than a thousand. Soon rats covered the entire town.

They squeezed under doors, climbed up drainpipes, and
fell in bunches down chimneys. The people tried, in vain,

to save some food, but the rats devoured everything.
Soon there was nothing left of the Christmas feast.

By Christmas morning, there were rats everywhere you looked: in cupboards, under beds, in shoes, in cradles.

The frightened people went to the town hall to demand
that the Mayor take action.

In an emergency meeting, the Mayor and his ministers came up with a plan to build traps and put out poison to rid Hamelin

of the rats. But these rats were too smart and too hardy. They avoided the traps and ate the poison as if it were candy.

On the third day, there wasn't enough food left in all of Hamelin to cook a single meal. But still the rats did not leave. They ate pillows, books, buttons, chairs, and tables.

They chased the dogs and killed the cats. They bit people in bed so that no one could sleep. When the people got out of bed and tried to get dressed, they found the rats had made nests in their shoes and hats. Finally, the desperate Mayor offered a thousand gold pieces to anyone who could rid the town of these pests.

On the fourth day, a stranger appeared in Hamelin. His clothes were brightly colored, and he wore a feather in his hat. He went to the town hall and asked to see the Mayor.

"I was told that you would pay a thousand gold pieces to anyone who rids Hamelin of rats," the stranger said.

"That is true, but who are you?" asked the Mayor.

"I am called the Pied Piper because of my colorful clothes. I know how to help you."

"Very well," the Mayor said. "If you can get rid of the rats, you will be paid the reward."

The Pied Piper left the town hall and walked to the marketplace. He began to play a strange melody on a simple wooden pipe. After only a few notes, all of the rats stopped eating to listen to the Piper's song. Then all at once, they ran from alleys, scampered out of houses, and dashed out of shops to gather around the Pied Piper.

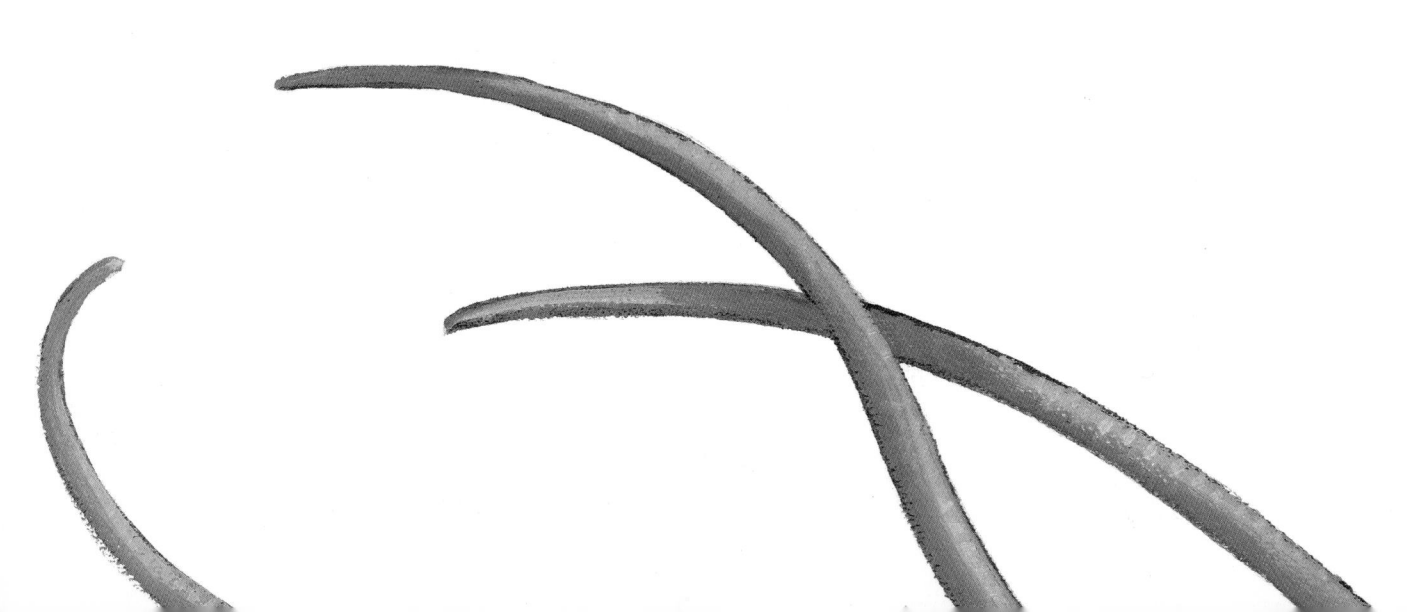

Soon the marketplace was filled with hundreds of thousands of rats. Still playing his pipe, the Piper began to

walk through the town. The rats followed as he led them
through the gates and out of Hamelin.

When he reached the edge of the river Weser, the Pied Piper stopped walking but kept playing his pipe. The rats continued running straight into

the river. By the time the Piper stopped playing,
every single rat in the town of Hamelin had been
swept away by the river.

The people ran out into the streets and sang and danced with joy. They rang the town bells to celebrate. But everyone had forgotten about the Pied Piper, and when he reappeared at the town gates, the Mayor's smile disappeared.

"I have done what I promised to do. Please give me the thousand gold pieces," the Piper said.

"Ah, yes," said the greedy Mayor. "You mean *fifty* gold pieces. Here they are."

"We agreed on a thousand, not fifty! Don't break your promise," said the Piper.

"Do you think we are going to give you a thousand gold pieces for playing a simple tune on your pipe? It's true that the rats are gone, but it required so little work. Now if you'd had to charm each rat separately, you would deserve the full reward. I offer you fifty gold pieces. Take them and leave!"

The Piper stared coldly at the Mayor. "You will regret this," he said, and left without the reward.

Weeks passed, and soon life in Hamelin returned to
the way it was before the rats. All the people remembered
of the Piper was that their shrewd Mayor had saved the

town a thousand gold pieces. Then one morning the townspeople heard the soft tones of a pipe, and they realized the Piper had returned.

As he played his strange and wonderful music, all the children of Hamelin gathered around him, singing,

laughing, and dancing. Their parents tried to hold them back, but their heads were filled with the Piper's song.

Without any fear, the children followed the Piper. In procession, they crossed the bridge over the river Weser and disappeared behind the mountains. The Pied Piper

and the children never returned to Hamelin. But ever since that time, when the wind blows from behind the mountains, you can hear the laughter of happy children.

AUTHOR'S NOTE

Hamelin, or Hameln, is a real town in Germany. In 1284, one hundred thirty children really did disappear from the town. No one knows what actually happened to them. Some historians think they left the town to join the famous Children's Crusade to reclaim Jerusalem from the Muslims. Others believe that because of overpopulation in Hamelin, a group of young people was sent away to colonize lands in eastern Europe. Although the origin of the Pied Piper legend is lost, Robert Browning popularized it with his poem "The Pied Piper of Hamelin" in 1842.